JASMÍN PICTURES HOME
JASMÍN ILUSTRA SU HOGAR

By Pedro Reyes, Yunior Jose Garcia,
Andy Pina, and Antonia Marisol Garcia

Illustrated by Ian L. Springer

Latin American Youth Center | Washington, DC

Shout Mouse Press

Latin American Youth Center /
Shout Mouse Press

Text copyright © 2021 by
Shout Mouse Press

Illustrations copyright © 2021
by Ian L. Springer

Design by Amber Colleran

Spanish translation by
Tatiana Figueroa Ramirez and Ártemis López

ISBN: 978-1-950807-41-3

Shout Mouse Press is a nonprofit writing and publishing program dedicated to amplifying underheard voices. Learn more and see our full catalog at www.shoutmousepress.org.

Shout Mouse Press
1638 R Street NW Suite 218
Washington, DC 20009

Trade distribution:
Ingram Book Group

For information about special discounts and bulk purchases, please contact Shout Mouse Press sales at 240-772-1545 or orders@shoutmousepress.org.

Acknowledgments

At Shout Mouse Press, we invite young people to write diverse and inclusive stories inspired by their own lived experiences. We believe that all children should be able to see themselves in the books they read, and that all children benefit from reading diverse perspectives on our shared world.

This book, written by young people from the Latin American Youth Center in Washington, DC, is born of this mission. These youth authors, ages 16-22, worked in teams of two to four to compose original children's books centering the hopes, dreams, joys, and challenges of being a young immigrant. They put their own hearts—and their personalities!—on the page, writing stories they hoped would inspire young readers to embrace who they are and to value the unique stories each one of us has to tell. These authors have our immense gratitude and respect: Mario, Jamileth, Tseganesh, Joy, Deyssy, Yenner, Andy, Marisol, Pedro, and Yunior.

This project represents a collaboration between Shout Mouse Press and the Latin American Youth Center (LAYC). From LAYC: Thanks to Cheili Obregon-Molina and Arisleidy Aquino for essential translation, collaboration, and positive energy, and to the LAYC program leadership of Julia Kann and Mike Leon. From Shout Mouse Press: We thank Programs Manager Alexa Patrick; Story Coaches Faith Campbell, Tatiana Figueroa Ramirez, and Barrett Smith; and Author Liaisons Rosa Reyes, Saylenis Palmore, Josselyn Mendoza, and Brenda Romero Peña for bringing fun and insight to the project. We can't thank enough illustrators Joy Ingram, Yurieli Otero-Asmar, Fatima Seck, and Ian Springer for bringing these stories to life with their beautiful artwork, and Amber Colleran for bringing a keen eye and important mentorship to the project as the series Art Director. Also muchísimas gracias are in order for Tatiana Figueroa Ramirez and Ártemis López for their thoughtful translation. We are grateful for the time and talents of these writers, mentors, and artists!

Finally, we are grateful to Today At Apple® Creative Studios DC, whose support made this project possible.

To all of the children from different countries:
always be proud of where you come from.

A todos los niños de diferentes países:
que siempre sientan orgullo del lugar de donde vienen.

Once there were four children who moved to a new town. They all loved soccer. They all spoke Spanish. And each one came from a different country.

Jorge, from Guatemala, liked to read, and Hector, from Mexico, loved music. There was Manolito, the little Dominican, who never got tired of eating. And finally there was Jasmín, from Honduras, who was always, ALWAYS drawing.

Una vez hubo cuatro niños que se mudaron a una nueva ciudad. A todos les encantaba el fútbol y todos hablaban español. Y cada uno vino de un país diferente.

A Jorge, de Guatemala, le gustaba leer; y Héctor, de México, amaba la música. Manolito, el pequeño dominicano, nunca se cansaba de comer. Y también estaba Jasmín, de Honduras, que siempre, SIEMPRE se la pasaba dibujando.

Jasmín was "the new one" at school. She didn't speak much English, only "hello" and "thank you." Jorge, Hector, and Manolito looked out for her, and served as her translators. They remembered what it was like being new.

Jasmín era "la nueva" en la escuela. No hablaba mucho inglés, solo "hola" y "gracias". Jorge, Héctor y Manolito la cuidaban y servían como traductores. Se acordaban de lo que era ser nuevo.

It wasn't easy, being new.

All the other students were born in the town and had known each other before they could walk.

The four friends always sat together in the cafeteria because they were the only ones who understood each other. Some days, they felt like an island in a wide sea.

No era fácil ser la nueva.

Todos los demás estudiantes nacieron en la ciudad y se conocían desde antes de que pudieran caminar.

Los cuatro amigos siempre se sentaban juntos en la cafetería porque eran los únicos que se entendían. Algunos días, se sentían como una isla en el ancho mar.

One day at lunch, while Manolito ate his rice, beans, and meat, and Hector sang made-up Mexican songs, and Jorge read his books, Jasmín sat quietly, drawing.

Un día durante el almuerzo, mientras
Manolito comía arroz, frijoles y carne; Héctor
cantaba canciones mexicanas inventadas y Jorge
leía sus libros; Jasmín dibujaba en silencio.

"Hey Jasmín, what are you drawing?" Manolito asked.

"Something for Culture Night. It's an assignment for art class."

Hector and Jorge looked over at Jasmín's notebook.

"A flower? Why does it look like that?" asked Jorge.

"Yeah. It looks really sad," said Hector.

"Because the flower is lonely," said Jasmín. "There are no other flowers like her."

—Oye, Jasmín, ¿qué estás dibujando? —preguntó Manolito.

—Algo para la Noche de la Cultura. Es una tarea para la clase de arte.

Héctor y Jorge miraron el cuaderno de Jasmín.

—¿Una flor? ¿Por qué se ve así? —preguntó Jorge.

—Simón. Se ve como que muy triste —dijo Héctor.

—Porque la flor se siente sola —dijo Jasmín—. No hay otras flores como ella.

"Is that flower you?" Jorge asked.

Jasmín lowered her head so that her hat covered her face. She said nothing.

"Jasmín, don't be sad," Hector said. "You have us."

"It's true," Manolito yelled, with a mouth full of rice. "You have us!"

"I know," said Jasmín quietly. "But…" She looked out at the other kids laughing and talking. "We are not like them…"

—¿Esa flor eres tú? —preguntó Jorge.

Jasmín bajó la cabeza para que su sombrero cubriera su rostro. No dijo nada.

—Jasmín, no estés triste —dijo Héctor—. Nos tienes a nosotros.

—Eso es —gritó Manolito, con la boca llena de arroz—. ¡Nos tienes a nosotros!

—Lo sé —dijo Jasmín en voz baja—. Pero… —miró a los otros niños, que se reían y hablaban entre sí—. No somos como ellos…

The boys looked at each other with concern.

"Exactly!" said Hector. "We are like us!"

"And we have amazing food!" said Manolito.

"And music!" said Hector. "And books!" said Jorge.

"Here," he continued, pushing his book towards her. "This book is all about Latin America. My grandpa gave it to me before I left. Maybe it can help you with ideas for your Culture Night assignment."

Jasmín raised her head and looked at the book out of the corner of her eye.

Los chicos se miraron con preocupación.

—¡Exacto! —dijo Héctor— ¡Somos como nosotros!

—¡Y tenemos comida increíble! —dijo Manolito.

—¡Y música! —dijo Héctor.

—¡Y libros! —dijo Jorge.

—Mira —añadió, mientras acercaba su libro hacia ella—. Este libro trata de Latinoamérica. Mi abuelo me lo dio antes de irme. Tal vez pueda darte ideas para tu tarea de la Noche de la Cultura.

Jasmín levantó la cabeza y miró el libro por el rabillo del ojo.

"Look, this is Guatemala," said Jorge. "We have many fields with large mountains and rubber trees everywhere! We eat tamales, empanadas, and mole like my grandmother made. Look at this photo here. These are the clothes we wear for our independence day. We dance to the Guatemalan sones and children play in the streets. I loved those days!"

"Let me see what it says about Mexico," Hector said.

〜

—Mira, esto es Guatemala —dijo Jorge—. Tenemos muchos campos con grandes montañas y árboles de hule por todas partes. Comemos tamales, empanadas y mole como hacía mi abuela. Mira esta foto aquí. Esta es la ropa que usamos para nuestro día de la independencia. Bailamos a los sones guatemaltecos los niños juegan en la calle. ¡Me encantaban esos días!

—Déjame ver qué dice sobre México —dijo Héctor.

"Mexico is a very diverse country that celebrates various traditions and festivals throughout its regions..." Jorge began to read.

Hector interrupted him. "In Mexico we have the January Party, where there are dances, fireworks, and taco vendors that fill the streets. The smell of the food makes you beg for more! And you can hear bands playing everywhere, and go on carnival rides!"

—México es un país muy diverso que celebra una gran variedad de tradiciones y festivales en todas sus regiones... —Jorge comenzó a leer.

Héctor lo interrumpió:

—En México tenemos la Fiesta de Enero, donde hay bailes, fuegos artificiales y vendedores de tacos que llenan las calles. ¡El olor de la comida hará que pidas más y más! ¡Y puedes escuchar bandas tocando en todas partes y participar en atracciones de carnaval!"

"Let me see that," said Manolito. "Here's the Dominican Republic! I miss the beaches, like the one in this photo. My favorite was Boca Chica, where there were street vendors selling coconut sticks, coconut water, and yaniqueques."

Manolito turned the page. "Look! Here is Carnival! The best part was when all of us ran from the vejigas. I loved that!"

"And you, Jasmín? What things do you miss about your country?" Manolito asked.

—Déjame ver —dijo Manolito—. ¡Aquí está la
República Dominicana! Echo de menos las playas, como
la de esta foto. Mi favorita era Boca Chica, donde había
vendedores ambulantes que vendían palitos de coco, agua
de coco y yaniqueques.

Manolito pasó la página:

—¡Mira! ¡Aquí está el Carnaval! Lo mejor fue correr de
las vejigas. ¡Me encantaba esa parte!

—¿Y tú, Jasmín? ¿Qué cosas extrañas de tu país? —
preguntó Manolito.

Jasmín flipped through the pages. "Well, I lived close to my family in Honduras — my parents, my grandmother, and all my cousins. We ate yummy food like baleadas, tripe soup, ticucos, montucas. There were cool places to visit, like the ruins of Copán, and lots of palm trees and beaches. I remember colorful parrots — like the one in this photo — and beautiful flowers that grew in the trees…"

"You know what? I have an idea!" yelled Jasmín, and she ran out of the cafeteria.

Jasmín ojeó las páginas:

—Bueno, vivía cerca de mi familia en Honduras: mis padres, mi abuela y todos mis primos. Comíamos comida deliciosa como baleadas, callos, ticucos, montucas… Había lugares interesantes para visitar, como las ruinas de Copán, y muchas palmeras y playas. Recuerdo loros coloridos, como el de esta foto, y hermosas flores que crecían en los árboles…

—¿Sabes qué? ¡Tengo una idea! —gritó Jasmín, y salió corriendo de la cafetería.

The children didn't see Jasmín for the rest of the day. They looked everywhere, but couldn't find her.

After school, when she showed up for soccer practice, her hands were painted in different colors and she was smiling from ear to ear.

The boys were half confused. "We have been looking for you," Manolito said.

"Oh, sorry. I was working on my Culture Night project!" Jasmín said. "You'll see…"

~

Los niños no vieron a Jasmín durante el resto del día. Buscaron por todas partes, pero no pudieron encontrarla.

Después de la escuela, cuando apareció para la práctica de fútbol, tenía las manos pintadas de diferentes colores y sonreía de oreja a oreja.

Los chicos estaban medio confundidos.

—Te estuvimos buscando, —dijo Manolito.

—Oh, lo siento. ¡Estaba trabajando en mi proyecto de la Noche de la Cultura! —dijo Jasmín—. Ya verán...

The next day was the Culture Night show. The boys came and saw paintings of the American flag, drawings of eagles, and even a hamburger sculpture!

Finally, they saw Jasmín, standing beside a huge beautiful painting. It was so full of color! And it held everything she had described about Honduras: the parrot, the palm trees, her family, everything. And right in the center was another flower, this one blooming and standing tall.

El día siguiente fue la Noche de la Cultura. Los niños vinieron y vieron pinturas de la bandera estadounidense, dibujos de águilas e incluso una escultura de una hamburguesa.

Finalmente, vieron a Jasmín, de pie junto a una enorme y hermosa pintura. ¡Era tan colorida! Y contenía todo lo que ella había descrito sobre Honduras: el loro, las palmeras, su familia, todo. Y justo en el centro había otra flor, pero esta floreciendo y erguida.

"WOWWW!" the boys exclaimed.

"It looks so pretty!"

"How did you do it?"

As people passed by, they stopped to admire Jasmín's art.

"Well, after talking to you, I realized that our memories of home are like art that we carry inside," said Jasmín. "And how beautiful it is to be from our countries! So to thank you, I made each of you a little present…

—¡WOWWW! —exclamaron los chicos.

—¡Se ve tan bonito!

—¿Cómo lo hiciste?

Mientras la gente pasaba, se detenían a admirar el arte de Jasmín.

—Bueno, después de hablar con ustedes, me di cuenta de que nuestros recuerdos del hogar son como el arte que llevamos adentro —dijo Jasmín—. ¡Y qué hermoso es ser de nuestros países! Así que para agradecerles, les hice un pequeño regalo a cada uno de ustedes…

… so that none of us ever forget."

... Para que ninguno de nosotros olvide nunca.

In this book, Jasmín draws her memories of home. What things remind you of home? Draw them here.

About the Illustrator

Ian L. Springer is an illustrator and sequential artist based in Silver Spring, MD. He is currently pursuing a BFA at Maryland Institute College of Art in Illustration with a concentration in Book Illustration. In addition to working as a freelance artist, he owns a digital art and entertainment e-commerce business, Immaculate Studios. He enjoys using narrative, words, and illustrations to convey stories and express a variety of characters and backgrounds. He works with many different digital mediums and is always looking to improve and adapt new stylistic approaches as an artist. You can view more of his work at is-studios.com.

Ian L. Springer es un ilustrador y artista secuencial basado en Silver Spring, MD. Actualmente trabaja en su licenciatura en Ilustración con una concentración en Ilustración de Libros en el Maryland Institute College of Art. Además de su trabajo como artista independiente, es dueño de un negocio de arte digital y entretenimiento, Immaculate Studios. Le gusta usar narrativa, palabras e ilustraciones para transmitir historias y expresar una variedad de personajes y raíces. Trabaja con muchos medios digitales distintos y siempre busca cómo puede mejorar y adaptar nuevas perspectivas estilísticas como artista. Puedes ver más de su trabajo en is-studios.com.

Writers and artists at work

About the Authors

Pedro Reyes, originally from Mexico, is 17 years old and studies at Cardozo High School. He decided to write this book because he believes it is a great experience to be part of something as big as writing a book. This story talks about love for our home countries, which he believes is very important.

Pedro Reyes, de origen mexicano y de 17 años, estudia en la Escuela Secundaria Cardozo. Decidió escribir este libro porque piensa que es una gran experiencia ser parte de algo tan grande como lo es escribir un libro. Este cuento habla del amor que le tenemos a nuestros países, lo cual él piensa que es muy importante.

Yunior Jose Garcia is 18 years old and from Guatemala. He is a student at Coolidge Senior High School and likes to play soccer. This is his first book. He decided to write this book because he wanted to have the experience of writing a children's book and to talk about different cultures. In the future, he would like to write a children's book about his life.

Yunior Jose Garcia tiene 18 años y es de Guatemala. Es un estudiante en la Escuela Secundaria Coolidge y le gusta jugar al fútbol. Este es su primer libro. Decidió escribir este libro porque le gustaría tener la experiencia de escribir libros para niños y para hablar de las diferentes culturas. En el futuro le gustaría escribir un libro para niños sobre su vida.

Tatiana Figuero served as Story Coach for this book, with **Saylenis Palmore** supporting.

Andy Pina is a 17 year old senior at Roosevelt High School, originally from the Dominican Republic. He likes to play video games, listen to music, and watch TV and online series. The reason why he wrote this book is because he wants kids not to feel ashamed of where they came from and for all kids to feel represented.

Andy Pina, de 17 años, está en su cuarto año en la Escuela Secundaria Roosevelt y es originario de la República Dominicana. Le gusta jugar videojuegos, escuchar música, y ver la televisión y series en línea. La razón por la cual él quiso escribir este libro es porque quiere que los niños no se sienten apenados de venir de dónde vinieron y para que todos los niños se sienten representados.

Antonia Marisol Garcia is 18 years old in level 1+2 at Next Step Public Charter School. She is originally from Honduras. During her free time, she likes to hang out with her friends. When she is older, she would like to work, travel, and buy a house. Marisol wrote this book because she wants to be a role model for others. She never thought she was going to be an author of a book! Marisol hopes that young people feel inspired when they read this book to know that their story matters, too.

Antonia Marisol Garcia tiene 18 años y es una estudiante de niveles 1 y 2 en la escuela Next Step. Es originaria de Honduras. Le gusta pasar su tiempo libre con sus amigos. Cuando sea mayor, le gustaría trabajar, viajar, y comprar una casa. Marisol escribió este libro porque quiere ser una inspiración para otros. ¡Nunca pensó que iba a ser autora de un libro! Marisol espera que los jóvenes se sientan inspirados cuando lean este libro para que sepan que sus historias también importan.

ABOUT LAYC

The Latin American Youth Center (LAYC) is a DC-based nonprofit organization that offers a variety of programming to low-income youth of all backgrounds. Their mission is to empower a diverse population of young people to achieve a successful transition to adulthood, through multicultural, comprehensive, and innovative programs that address youths' social, academic, and career needs.

El Latin American Youth Center (LAYC) es una organización sin fines de lucro con sede en Washington, DC que ofrece una variedad de programas para jóvenes de bajos recursos de todos los orígenes. Su misión consiste en capacitar a una población diversa de jóvenes para que logren una transición exitosa a la edad adulta a través de programas multiculturales, integrales e innovadores que abordan las necesidades sociales, académicas y profesionales de la juventud.

Learn more at layc-dc.org

ABOUT SHOUT MOUSE PRESS

Shout Mouse Press is a nonprofit organization dedicated to centering and amplifying the voices of marginalized youth (ages 12+) via writing workshops, publication, and public speaking opportunities. The young people we coach are underrepresented—as characters and as creators—within young people's literature, and their perspectives underheard. Our work provides a platform for them to tell their own stories and, as published authors, to act as leaders and agents of change.

Shout Mouse Press es una organización sin fines de lucro dedicada a centrar y amplificar las voces de los jóvenes marginalizados (a partir de los 12 años) a través de talleres de escritura, publicación, y oportunidades para hablar en público. La gente joven a la que entrenamos está subrepresentada—como personajes y como creadores—en la literatura para gente joven, y sus perspectivas son poco escuchadas. Nuestro trabajo les proporciona una plataforma para contar sus propias historias y, como autores publicados, actuar como líderes y agentes de cambio.

Learn more at shoutmousepress.org

MORE BOOKS FROM SHOUT MOUSE PRESS

Shout Mouse Press is passionate about letting young people speak for themselves—and making sure they are heard. We lead writing and art workshops that center youth voices, then edit and design their books, and finally publish and promote their important work. We ensure that earned income from book sales is invested directly back into young people themselves: proceeds support scholarship funds for author communities, salaries for author interns, and programs that help young people speak up, be heard, and be taken seriously as leaders in their community.

Check out our catalogue of 50+ award-winning youth-authored titles including children's books, graphic novels, novels, memoirs, and poetry collections at **shoutmousepress.org**.

WHERE TO BUY

We encourage you to order books directly through Shout Mouse Press online in order to best benefit our authors. For bulk orders, educator inquiries, and nonprofit discounts: email **orders@shoutmousepress.org**.

Books are also available through Amazon, Bookshop.org, and other online retailers.

Shout Mouse titles are distributed by Ingram.

OTHER WAYS TO ENGAGE

Shout Mouse Press can bring speakers to your class or event. Call us at 240-772-1545 or request via **shoutmousepress.org/ request-an-author-talk**.

Support our youth writing and publishing programs by becoming a donor: **shoutmousepress.org/donate**.

OUR IMPACT

90,000+
Shout Mouse books in circulation

8
National Literary Awards, including 4 Book of the Year Designations

$140,000+
raised in scholarship funds for author communities

20,000+
audience members reached through 100+ Author Talks in schools, libraries, and conferences

20,000+
books donated to young readers in need

VOCES SIN FRONTERAS

As immigrants and activists, the Latino Youth Leadership Council of LAYC recognized the urgent need for #OwnVoices stories to provide a human face to the U.S. immigration debate. With few youth-focused books reflecting their personal narratives, they decided to boldly share their own. The Shout Mouse team of teaching artists and comic coaches worked with these youth leaders to share their memoirs about immigrating to the U.S., and now educators across the country are using their stories to educate, affirm, and inspire their students. For ages 12+.

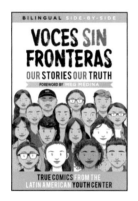

Voces Sin Fronteras: Our Stories, Our Truth
978-1945434921

Voces Sin Fronteras is a bilingual collection of 16 self-illustrated graphic memoirs by teen immigrants from Central America and the Caribbean. These thought-provoking and powerfully honest stories address themes of poverty, family, grief, education, and, of course, the pain and promise of immigration. This book is an opportunity to hear directly from youth who are often in the headlines but whose stories don't get told in full. Foreword by Newbery Medal winner Meg Medina.

"When I tell my story, it heals what it is in my past.... If you never share, the pain will never leave, it will always be there... [Telling your story] will help you to heal inside, to be who you are, to speak out."

— Erminia, co-author of *Voces Sin Fronteras*, on the power of sharing her story via Author Talks

REVIEWS

"This powerful compendium amplifies teens' understanding of the young immigrant experience— facing fears, overcoming sadness, learning a new language, and being left by parents who migrated first, then forgiving and reuniting with them decades later... VERDICT: Spotlighting underrepresented voices, this work is highly recommended for all communities in their efforts to promote empathetic, inclusive discussions around immigration."
—*School Library Journal*, Starred Review

"The compelling stories shared by these students… signal their desire to serve as beacons or lifelines for other young immigrants. Their testimonies, as Newbery Medal winner Meg Medina points out in her foreword, are ultimately about courage… Enlightening and inspiring #ownvoices accounts by young activists."   — Kirkus Reviews

AWARDS

2020 International Latino Book Awards
Best Young Adult Nonfiction

2019 "In the Margins"
Top Nonfiction Prize

Made in the USA
Middletown, DE
14 November 2021